The Whistling